The Dre
BALSO SNELL

Nathanael West

DOVER PUBLICATIONS, INC.
Mineola, New York

Bibliographical Note

This Dover edition, first published in 2004, is an unabridged republication of the work originally published in 1931 by Moss & Kamin, New York.

Library of Congress Cataloging-in-Publication Data

West, Nathanael, 1903–1940.
    The dream life of Balso Snell / Nathanael West.
        p. cm.
    ISBN 0-486-43389-7 (pbk.)
    I. Title.

PS3545.E8334D7 2004
813'.52—dc22

2003063498

Manufactured in the United States of America
Dover Publications, Inc., 31 East 2nd Street, Mineola, N.Y. 11501

To A.S.

"After all, my dear fellow, life,
Anaxagoras has said, is a journey."

—BERGOTTE

While walking in the tall grass that has sprung up around the city of Troy, Balso Snell came upon the famous wooden horse of the Greeks. A poet, he remembered Homer's ancient song and decided to find a way in.

On examining the horse, Balso found that there were but three openings: the mouth, the navel, and the posterior opening of the alimentary canal. The mouth was beyond his reach, the naval proved a cul-de-sac, and so, forgetting his dignity, he approached the last. O Anus Mirabilis!

Along the lips of the mystic portal he discovered writings which after a little study he was able to decipher. Engraved in a heart pierced by an arrow and surmounted by the initial N, he read, "Ah! Qualis . . . Artifex . . . Pereo!" Not to be outdone by the actor-emperor, Balso carved with his penknife another heart and the words "O Byss! O Abyss! O Anon! O Anan!" omitting, however, the arrow and his initial.

Before entering he prayed:

"O Beer! O Meyerbeer! O Bach! O Offenbach! Stand me now as ever in good stead."

Balso immediately felt like the One at the Bridge, the Two in the Bed, the Three in the Boat, the Four on Horseback, the Seven Against Thebes. And with a high heart he entered the gloom of the foyer-like lower intestine.

1

After a little while, seeing no one and hearing nothing, Balso began to feel depressed. To keep his heart high and yet out of his throat, he made a song.

> Round as the Anus
> Of a Bronze Horse
> Or the Tender Buttons
> Used by Horses for Ani
>
> On the Wheels of His Car
> Ringed Round with Brass
> Clamour the Seraphim
> Tongues of Our Lord
>
> Full Ringing Round
> As the Belly of Silenus
> Giotto Painter of Perfect Circles
> Goes . . . One Motion Round
>
> Round and Full
> Round and Full as
> A Brimming Goblet
> The Dew-Loaded Navel
> Of Mary
> Of Mary Our Mother
>
> Round and Ringing Full
> As the Mouth of a Brimming Goblet
> The Rust-Laden Holes
> In Our Lord's Feet.
> Entertain the Jew-Driven Nails.

He later gave this song various names, the most successful of which were: *Anywhere Out of the World, or a Voyage Through the Hole in the Mundane Millstone* and *At Hoops with the Ani of Bronze Horses, or Toe Holes for a Flight of Fancy.*

But despite the gaiety of his song, Balso did not feel sure of himself. He thought of the Phoenix Excrementi, a race of men he had invented one Sunday afternoon while in bed, and trembled, thinking he might well meet one in this place. And he had good cause to tremble, for the Phoenix Excrementi eat themselves, digest themselves, and give birth to themselves by evacuating their bowels.

Hoping to attract the attention of an inhabitant, Balso shouted as though overwhelmed by the magnificence of his surroundings:

"O the Rose Gate! O the Moist Garden! O Well! O Fountain! O Sticky Flower! O Mucous Membrane!"

A man with "Tours" embroidered on his cap stalked out of the shadow. In order to prove a poet's right to trespass, Balso quoted from his own works:

"If you desire to have two parallel lines meet at once or even in the near future," he said, "it is important to make all the necessary arrangements beforehand, preferably by wireless."

The man ignored his little speech. "Sir," he said, "you are an ambassador from that ingenious people, the inventors and perfectors of the automatic water-closet, to my people who are the heirs of Greece and Rome. As your own poet has so well put it, 'The Grandeur that was Greece and the Glory that was Rome' . . . I offer you my services as guide. First you will please look to the right where you will see a beautiful Doric prostate gland swollen with gladness and an over-abundance of good cheer."

This speech made Balso very angry. "Inventors of the automatic water-closet, are we?" he shouted. "Oh, you stinker! Doric, bah! It's Baptist '68, that's what it is. And no prostate gland either, simply an atrophied pile. You call this dump grand and glorious, do you? Have you ever seen the Grand Central Station, or the Yale Bowl, or the Holland

Tunnel, or the New Madison Square Garden? Exposed plumbing, stinker, that's all I see—and at this late date. It's criminally backward, do you hear me?"

The guide gave ground before Balso's rage. "Please sir," he said, "please . . . After all, the ages have sanctified this ground, great men have hallowed it. In Rome do as the Romans do."

"Stinker," Balso repeated, but less ferociously this time.

The guide took heart. "Mind your manners, foreigner. If you don't like it here, why don't you go back where you came from? But before you go let me tell you a story—an old tale of my people, rich in local color. And, you force me to say it, apropos, timely. However, let me assure you that I mean no offense. The title of the story is

"VISITORS

"A traveler in Tyana, who was looking for the sage Appolonius, saw a snake enter the lower part of a man's body. Approaching the man, he said:

"'Pardon me, my good fellow, but a snake just entered your . . .' He finished by pointing.

"'Yes sir, he lives there,' was the astounding rejoinder.

"'Ah, then you must be the man I'm looking for, the philosopher-saint, Appolonius of Tyana. Here is a letter of introduction from my brother George. May I see the snake please? Now the opening. Perfect!'"

Balso echoed the last word of the story. "Perfect! Perfect! A real old-world fable. You may consider yourself hired."

"I have other stories to tell," the guide said, "and I shall tell them as we go along. By the way, have you heard the one about Moses and the Burning Bush? How the prophet rebuked the Bush for speaking by quoting the proverb, 'Good wine needs no bush'; and how the Bush insolently replied, 'A hand in the Bush is worth two in the pocket.'"

Balso did not consider this story nearly as good as the other; in fact he thought it very bad, yet he was determined to make no more breaks and entered the large intestine on the arm of his guide. He let the guide do all the talking and they made great headway up the tube. But, unfortunately, coming suddenly upon a place where the intestine had burst through the stomach wall, Balso cried out in amazement:

"What a hernia! What a hernia!"

The guide began to splutter with rage and Balso tried to pacify him by making believe he had not meant the scenery. "Hernia," he said, rolling the word on his tongue. "What a pity childish associations cling to beautiful words such as hernia, making their use as names impossible. Hernia! What a beautiful name for a girl! Hernia Hornstein! Paresis Pearlberg! Paranoia Puntz! How much more pleasing to the ear [and what other sense should a name please?] than Faith Rabinowitz or Hope Hilkowitz."

But Balso had only blundered again. "Sirrah!" the guide cried in an enormous voice, "I am a Jew! and whenever anything Jewish is mentioned, I find it necessary to say that I am a Jew. I'm a Jew! A Jew!"

"Oh, you mistake me," Balso said, "I have nothing against the Jews. I admire the Jews; they are a thrifty race. Some of my best friends are Jews." But his protests availed him little until he thought to quote C. M. Doughty's epigram. "The semites," Balso said with great firmness, "are like to a man sitting in a cloaca to the eyes, and whose brows touch heaven."

When Balso had at last succeeded in quieting the guide, he tried to please him further by saying that the magnificent tunnel stirred him to the quick and that he would be satisfied to spend his remaining days in it with but a few pipes and a book.

The guide tossed up his arms in one of those eloquent gestures the latins know so well how to perform and said:

"After all, what is art? I agree with George Moore. Art is not nature, but rather nature digested. Art is a sublime excrement."

"And Daudet?" Balso queried.

"Oh, Daudet! Daudet, c'est de bouillabaisse! You know, George Moore also says, 'What care I that the virtue of some sixteen-year-old maiden was the price paid for Ingres' La Source?' Now . . ."

"Picasso says," Balso broke in, "Picasso says there are no feet in nature . . . And, thanks for showing me around. I have to leave."

But before he was able to get away, the guide caught him by the collar. "Just a minute, please. You were right to interrupt. We should talk of art, not artists. Please explain your interpretation of the Spanish master's dictum."

"Well, the point is . . ." Balso began. But before he could finish the guide started again. "If you are willing to acknowledge the existence of points," he said, "then the statement that there are no feet in nature puts you in an untenable position. It depends for its very meaning on the fact that there are no points. Picasso, by making this asser-tion, has placed himself on the side of monism in the eter-nal wrangle between the advocates of the Singular and those of the Plural. As James puts it, 'Does reality exist dis-tributively or collectively—in the shape of *eaches, everys, anys, eithers* or only in the shape of an *all* or *whole*?' If reality is singular then there are no feet in nature, if plur-al, a great many. If the world is one [everything part of the same thing—called by Picasso nature] then nothing either begins or ends. Only when things take the shapes of *eaches, everys, anys, eithers* [have ends] do they have feet. Feet are attached to ends, by definition. Moreover, if everything is one, and has neither ends nor beginnings, then everything is a circle. A circle has neither a beginning nor an end. A circle has no feet. If we believe that nature is a circle, then we must also believe that there are no feet in nature.

"Do not pooh-pooh this idea as mystical. Bergson has . . ."

"Cezanne said, 'Everything tends toward the globular.'" With this announcement Balso made another desperate attempt to escape.

"Cezanne?" the guide said, keeping a firm hold on Balso's collar. "Cezanne is right. The sage of Aix is . . ."

With a violent twist, Balso tore loose and fled.

Balso fled down the great tunnel until he came upon a man, naked except for a derby in which thorns were sticking, who was attempting to crucify himself with thumb tacks. His curiosity got the better of his fear and he stopped.

"Can I help you?" he asked politely.

"No," the man answered with even greater politeness, tipping his hat repeatedly as he spoke. "No, I can manage, thank you . . .

"My name is Maloney the Areopagite," the man continued, answering the questions Balso was too well-bred to word, "and I am a catholic mystic. I believe implicitly in that terrible statement of Saint Hildegarde's, 'The lord dwells not in the bodies of the healthy and vigorous.' I live as did Marie Alacoque, Suso, Labre, Lydwine of

Schiedam, Rose of Lima. When my suffering is not too severe, I compose verses in imitation of Notker Balbus, Ekkenard le Vieux, Hucbald le Chauve.

> "In the feathered darkness
> Of thy mouth,
> O Mother of God!
> I worship Christ
> The culminating rose.

"Get the idea? I spend the rest of my time marveling at the love shown by all the great saints for even the lowliest of God's creatures. Have you ever heard of Benedict Labre? It was he who picked up the vermin that fell out of his hat and placed them piously back into his sleeve. Before calling in a laundress, another very holy man removed the vermin from his clothes in order not to drown the jewels of sanctity infesting them.

"Inspired by these thoughts I have decided to write the biography of Saint Puce, a great martyred member of the vermin family. If you are interested, I will give you a short précis of his life."

"Please do so, sir," Balso said. "Live and learn is my motto, Mr. Maloney, so please continue."

"Saint Puce was a flea," Maloney the Areopagite began in a well-trained voice. "A flea who was born, lived, and died, beneath the arm of our Lord.

"Saint Puce was born from an egg that was laid in the flesh of Christ while as a babe He played on the floor of the stable in Bethlehem. That the flesh of a god has been a stage in the incubation of more than one being is well known: Dionysius and Athene come to mind.

"Saint Puce had two mothers: the winged creature that laid the egg, and the God that hatched it in His flesh. Like most of us, he had two fathers: our Father Who art in

Heaven, and he who in the cocksureness of our youth we called 'pop.'

"Which of his two fathers fertilized the egg? I cannot answer with certainty, but the subsequent actions of Saint Puce's life lead me to believe that the egg was fertilized by a being whose wings were of feathers. Yes, I mean the Dove or Paraclete—the Sanctus Spiritus. In defense of this belief antiquity will help us again: it is only necessary to remember Leda and Europa. And I must remind you, you who might plead a puce too small physically, of the nature of God's love and how it embraceth all.

"O happy, happy childhood! Playing in the curled brown silk, sheltered from all harm by Christ's arm. Eating the sweet flesh of our Saviour; drinking His blood; bathing in His sweat; partaking, oh how fully! of His Godhead. Having no need to cry as I have cried:

"Corpus Christi, salva me
Sanguis Christi, inebria me
Aqua lateris Christi, lave me.

"In manhood, fullgrown, how strong Saint Puce was, how lusty; and how his lust and strength were satisfied in one continuous, never-culminating ecstasy. The music of our Lord's skin sliding over His flesh!—more exact than the fugues of Bach. The pattern of His veins!—more intricate than the Maze at Cnossos. The odors of His Body!—more fragrant than the Temple of Solomon. The temperature of His flesh!—more pleasant than the Roman baths to the youth Puce. And, finally, the taste of His blood! In this wine all pleasure, all excitement, was magnified, until with ecstasy Saint Puce's small body roared like a furnace.

"In his prime, Saint Puce wandered far from his birthplace, that hairsilk pocketbook, the armpit of our Lord. He roamed the forest of God's chest and crossed the hill of His abdomen. He measured and sounded that fathomless well, the Navel of our Lord. He explored and charted every crevasse, ridge, and cavern of Christ's body. From notes taken during his travels he later wrote his great work, *A Geography of Our Lord.*

"After much wandering, tired, he returned at last to his home in the savoury forest. To spend, he thought, his remaining days in writing, worship, and contemplation. Happy in a church whose walls were the flesh of Christ, whose windows were rose with the blood of Christ, and on whose altars burned golden candles made of the sacred earwax.

"Soon, too soon, alas! the day of martyrdom arrived [O Jesu, mi dulcissime!], and the arms of Christ were lifted that His hands might receive the nails.

"The walls and windows of Saint Puce's church were broken and its halls flooded with blood.

"The hot sun of Calvary burnt the flesh beneath Christ's upturned arm, making the petal-like skin shrivel until it looked like the much-shaven armpit of an old actress.

"After Christ died, Saint Puce died, refusing to desert to lesser flesh, even to that of Mary who stood close under the cross. With his last strength he fought off the unconquerable worm. . . ."

Mr. Maloney's thin frame was racked by sobs as he finished, yet Balso did not spare him.

"I think you're morbid," he said. "Don't be morbid. Take your eyes off your navel. Take your head from under your armpit. Stop sniffing mortality. Play games. Don't read so many books. Take cold showers. Eat more meat."

With these helpful words, Balso left him to his own devices and continued on his way.

✲

THE DREAM LIFE OF BALSO SNELL

He had left Maloney the Areopagite far behind when, on
turning a bend in the intestine, he saw a boy hiding what
looked like a packet of letters in a hollow tree. After the
boy had left, Balso removed the packet and sat down to
read. First, however, he took off his shoes because his feet
hurt.

What he had taken for letters proved on closer scrutiny
to be a diary. At the top of the first page was written,
"English Theme by John Gilson, Class 8B, Public School
186, Miss McGeeney, teacher." He read further.

Jan. 1st—at home

Whom do I fool by calling these pages a journal? Surely
not you, Miss McGeeney. Alas! no-one. Nor is anyone
fooled by the fact that I write in the first person. It is for
this reason that I do not claim to have found these pages in
a hollow tree. I am an honest man and feel badly about
masks, cardboard noses, diaries, memoirs, letters from a
Sabine farm, the theatre . . . I feel badly, yet I can do nothing. 'Sir!' I say to myself, 'your name is not Iago, but simply John. It is monstrous to write lies in a diary.'

However, I insist that I am an honest man. Reality troubles me as it must all honest men.

Reality! Reality! If I could only discover the Real. A Real
that I could know with my senses. A Real that would wait
for me to inspect it as a dog inspects a dead rabbit. But,
alas! when searching for the Real I throw a stone into a
pool whose ripples become of advancing less importance
until they are too large for connection with, or even memory of, the stone agent.

*Written while smelling the moistened forefinger of my left
hand.*

Jan. 2nd—at home

Is this journal to be like all the others I have started? A

large first entry, consisting of the incident which made me think my life exciting enough to keep a journal, followed by a series of entries gradually decreasing in size and culminating in a week of blank days.

Inexperienced diary-writers make their first entry the largest. They come to the paper with a constipation of ideas—eager, impatient. The white paper acts as a laxative. A diarrhoea of words is the result. The richness of the flow is unnatural; it cannot be sustained.

A diary must grow naturally—a flower, a cancer, a civilization . . . In a diary there is no need for figures of speech, honest Iago.

Sometimes my name is Raskolnikov, sometimes it is Iago. I never was, and never shall be, plain John Gilson— honest, honest Iago, yes, but never honest John. As Raskolnikov, I keep a journal which I call *The Making of a Fiend*. I give the heart of my Crime Journal:

Crime Journal

I have been in this hospital seven weeks. I am under observation. Am I sane? This diary shall prove me insane.

This entry gives me away.

Crime Journal

My mother visited me today. She cried. It is she who is crazy. Order is the test of sanity. Her emotions and thoughts are disordered. Mine are arranged, valued, placed.

Man spends a great deal of time making order out of chaos, yet insists that the emotions be disordered. I order my emotions: I am insane. Yet sanity is discipline. My mother rolls on the hospital floor and cries: "John darling . . . John sweetheart." Her hat falls over her face. She clutches her absurd bag of oranges. She is sane.

I say to her quietly: "Mother, I love you, but this spectacle is preposterous—and the smell of your clothing depresses me." I am insane.

Crime Journal

Order is vanity. I have decided to discard the nonsense of precision instruments. No more measuring. I drop the slide rule and take up the Golden Rule. Sanity is the absence of extremes.

Crime Journal

Is someone reading my diary while I sleep?

On reading what I have written, I think I can detect a peculiar change in my words. They have taken on the quality of comment.

You who read these pages while I sleep, please sign your name here.

John Raskolnikov Gilson

Crime Journal

During the night I got up, turned to yesterday's entry and signed my name.

Crime Journal

I am insane. I [the papers had it CULTURED FIEND SLAYS DISHWASHER] am insane.

When a baby, I affected all the customary poses: I "laughed the icy laughter of the soul," I uttered "universal sighs"; I sang in "silver-fire verse"; I smiled the "enigmatic smile"; I sought "azure and elliptical routes." In everything I was completely the mad poet. I was one of those "great despisers," whom Nietzche loved because "they are the great adorers; they are arrows of longing for the other shore." Along with "mon hysterie" I cultivated a "rotten, ripe maturity." You understand what I mean: like Rimbaud, I practiced having hallucinations.

Now, my imagination is a wild beast that cries always for

freedom. I am continually tormented by the desire to indulge some strange thing, perceptible but indistinct, hidden in the swamps of my mind. This hidden thing is always crying out to me from its hiding-place: "Do as I tell you and you will find out my shape. There, quick! what is that thing in your brain? Indulge my commands and some day the great doors of your mind will swing open and allow you to enter and handle to your complete satisfaction the vague shapes and figures hidden there."

I can know nothing; I can have nothing; I must devote my whole life to the pursuit of a shadow. It is as if I were attempting to trace with the point of a pencil the shadow of the tracing pencil. I am enchanted with the shadow's shape and want very much to outline it; but the shadow is attached to the pencil and moves with it, never allowing me to trace its tempting form. Because of some great need, I am continually forced to make the attempt.

Two years ago I sorted books for eight hours a day in the public library. Can you imagine how it feels to be surrounded for eight long hours by books—a hundred billion words one after another according to ten thousand mad schemes. What patience, what labor are those crazy sequences the result of! What starving! What sacrifice! And the fervors, deliriums, ambitions, dreams, that dictated them! . . .

The books smelt like the breaths of their authors; the books smelt like a closet full of old shoes through which a steam pipe passes. As I handled them they seemed to turn into flesh, or at least some substance that could be eaten.

Have you ever spent any time among the people who farm the great libraries: the people who search old issues of the medical journals for pornography and facts about strange diseases; the comic writers who exhume jokes from old magazines; the men and women employed by the insurance companies to gather statistics on death? I worked in the philosophy department. That department is patronized by alchemists, astrologers, cabalists, demonologists, magicians, atheists, and the founders of new religious systems.

While working in the library, I lived in a theatrical rooming house in the west Forties, a miserable, uncomfortable place. I lived there because of the discomfort. I wanted to be miserable. I could not have lived in a comfortable house. The noises [harsh, grating], the dirt [animal, greasy], the smells [dry sweat, sour mold], permitted me to wallow in my discomfort. My mind was full of vague irritations and annoyances. My body was nervous and jumpy, and demanded an extraordinary amount of sleep. I was a bundle of physical and mental tics. I climbed into myself like a bear into a hollow tree, and lay there long hours, overpowered by the heat, odor, and nastiness of I.

The only other person living on my floor, the top one, was an idiot. He earned his living as a dishwasher in the kitchen of the Hotel Astor. He was a fat, pink and grey pig of a man, and stank of stale tobacco, dry perspiration, clothing mold, and oatmeal soap. He did not have a skull on the top of his neck, only a face; his head was all face— a face without side, back or top, like a mask.

The idiot never wore a collar, yet he kept both a front and a back collar button in the neckband of his shirt. When he changed his shirt he removed the collar buttons from the dirty shirt and placed them in the clean one. His neck was smooth, white, fat, and covered all over with tiny blue veins like a piece of cheap marble. His Adam's apple was very large and looked as though it might be a soft tumor in his throat. When he swallowed, his neck bulged out and he made a sound like a miniature toilet being flushed.

My neighbor, the idiot, never smiled, but laughed

continually. It must have hurt him to laugh. He fought his laughter as though it were a wild beast. A beast of laughter seemed always struggling to escape from between his teeth.

People say that it is terrible to hear a man cry. I think it is even worse to hear a man laugh. [Yet the ancients considered hysteria a woman's disease. They believed that hysteria was caused by the womb breaking loose and floating freely through the body. The cure they practiced was to place sweet-smelling herbs to the vulva in order to attract the womb back to its original position, and foul-smelling things to the nose in order to keep the womb away from the head.]

One night at the movies, I heard a basso from the Chicago Opera Company sing the devil's serenade from Faust. A portion of this song calls for a long laugh. When the singer came to the laugh he was unable to get started. He struggled with the laugh, but it refused to come. At last he managed to start laughing. Once started, he was unable to stop. The orchestra repeated the transition that led from the laugh to the next bars of the song, but he was unable to stop laughing.

I returned home with my head full of the singer's laughter. Because of it I was unable to fall asleep. I dressed myself and went downstairs. On my way to the street I passed my neighbor the idiot. He was laughing to himself. His laughter made me laugh. When he detected the strain in my voice he grew angry. He thought that I was making fun of him. He said, "Who you laughing at?" I became frightened and offered him a cigarette. He refused it. I left him on the stairs, struggling with his laughter and his anger.

I knew that if I did not get my customary amount of sleep, I would suffer when the time came for me to get up.

I was certain that if I went back to bed I would be unable to sleep. In order to tire myself as quickly as possible, I walked to Broadway and then started uptown. My shoes hurt me and at first I enjoyed the pain. Soon, however, the pain became so intense that I had to stop walking and return home.

On regaining my bed, I still found it impossible to fall asleep. I knew that I must become interested in something outside of myself or go insane. I plotted the death of the idiot.

I felt certain that it would be a safe murder to commit. Safe, because its motives would not be comprehensible to the police. Policemen are reasonable men; they do not consider the shape and color of a man's throat, his laugh or the fact that he does not wear a collar, reasonable motives for killing him.

You also, eh, doctor, consider these poor reasons for murder. I agree—they are literary reasons. Reasoning your way, dear doctor—like Darwin or a policeman—I am expected to trace my action back to some such things as the desire to live or create life. Because I want you to believe me, I shall say that in order to remain sane I had to kill this man, just as I had to kill, when a child, all the flies in my room before being able to fall asleep.

Nonsense, eh? I agree—nonsense. Please, please—here [please believe me] is why I killed Adolph. I killed the idiot because he disturbed my sense of balance. I killed him thinking his death would permit me to regain my balance. My beloved balance!

The fact that I had never killed made me uncomfortable. What was this enormous crime I had never committed? What were all the horrors attendant on this act? I killed a man and discovered the answers. I shall never kill another man. I shall never need to kill another man.

Let me continue with my confession. I decided not to plot an intricate killing. I was afraid that if I attempted a complicated crime I might get entangled in my own scheme. I decided to have the murder consist of only one act, the killing. I even resisted the desire to look up certain books in the library.

Because the idea of the killing involved the dishwasher's throat, I decided to do the job with a knife. As a child I always took pleasure in cutting soft, firm things. I purchased a knife about fifteen inches long. The knife had only one cutting edge; the other edge or the back of the knife was about half an inch thick. Its weight made it a perfect instrument for the job.

I did not want to commit the murder too soon after purchasing the knife; but on the very night that I brought it home, I heard the idiot come up the stairs drunk. As I listened to him fumble with his key, I realized, for the first time, that he locked his door at night. This unlooked-for obstacle almost made me give up the idea of killing him. I rid myself of my misgivings by thinking of the torture I would have to go through if I frustrated my desire to commit murder. I decided to do the job that very evening and have it over with. I put on my bathrobe and went into the hall. His door was ajar. I went to it carefully. The idiot was stretched out on his bed, drunk. I went back to my room and took off my bathrobe and pajamas. I planned to do the murder naked, so that I should have no blood-stained things to wash or destroy. What blood I got on my body I could easily wash off. Naked: I felt cold; and I noticed that my genitals were tight and hard, like a dog's, or an archaic Greek statue's—they were as though I had just come out of an ice-cold bath. I was aware of a great excitement; an excitement that seemed to be near, but not quite within me.

I crossed the hall and entered the dishwasher's room. He had left his light burning. I walked to him and cut his throat. I had intended to do the cutting with several rapid strokes, but he awoke at the touch of the steel and I became frightened and sawed at his throat in a panic. When he lay still I calmed down.

I went back to my room and stood the knife up in the sink, like one does a wet umbrella, letting what blood was on it run into the drain. I dressed quickly, obsessed by the need for getting rid of the knife. While dressing I became conscious of a growing fear. A fear that as it grew seemed likely to burst me open; a fear so large that I felt I could not contain it without rupturing my mind. Inside of my head this expanding fear was like a rapidly growing child inside the belly of a mother. I felt that I must get rid of the fear or burst. I opened my mouth wide, but I was unable to give birth to my fear.

Carrying this fear as an ant carries a caterpiller thirty times its size, I ran down the stairs and into the street. I hurried west toward the river.

I let the knife slip into the water. With the knife went my fear. I felt light and free. I felt like a happy girl. I said to myself: "You feel like a young girl—kittenish, cuney-cutey, darlingey, springtimey." I caressed my breasts like a young girl who has suddenly become conscious of her body on a hot afternoon. I imitated the mannered walk of a girl showing off before a group of boys. In the dark I hugged myself.

On my way back to Broadway I passed some sailors, and felt an overwhelming desire to flirt with them. I went through all the postures of a desperate prostitute; I camped for all I was worth. The sailors looked at me and laughed. I wanted very much for one of them to follow me. Suddenly I heard the sound of footsteps behind me. The steps came close and I felt as though I were melting—all silk and perfumed, pink lace. I died the little death. But the man went past without noticing me. I sat down on a bench and was violently sick.

I sat on the bench for a long time, and then returned to my room, sick and cold.

Inside of my head the murder has become like a piece of sand inside the shell of an oyster. My mind has commenced to form a pearl around it. The idiot, the singer, his laugh, the knife, the river, my change of sex, all cover the murder just as the secretions of an oyster cover an irritating grain of sand. As the accumulations grow and become solidified, the original irritation disappears. If the murder continues to grow in size it may become too large for me to contain; then I am afraid it will kill me, just as the pearl eventually kills the oyster.

Balso put the manuscript back into the tree and continued on his way, his head bowed in thought. The world was getting to be a difficult place for a lyric poet. He felt old. "Ah youth!" he sighed elaborately. "Ah Balso Snell!"

Suddenly he heard a voice at his elbow.

"Well, nosey, how did you like my theme?"

Balso turned and saw the boy whose diary he had been reading. He was still in short pants and looked less than twelve years old.

"Interesting psychologically, but is it art?" Balso said timidly. "I'd give you B minus and a good spanking."

"What the hell do I care about art! Do you know why I wrote that ridiculous story—because Miss McGeeney, my English teacher, reads Russian novels and I want to sleep with her. But maybe you run a magazine. Will you buy it? I need money."

"No, son, I'm a poet. I'm Balso Snell, the poet."

"A poet! For Christ's sake!"

"What you ought to do, child, is to run about more. Read less and play baseball."

"Forget it. I know a fat girl who only sleeps with poets. When I'm with her I'm a poet, too. I won her with a poem.

"O Beast of Walls!
O Walled-in Fat Girl!
Your conquest was hardly worth
The while of one whom Arras and
Arrat, Pelion, Ossa, Parnassus, Ida,
Pisgah and Pike's Peak never in-
terested.

"Not bad, eh? But I'm fed up with poetry and art. Yet what can I do. I need women and because I can't buy or force them, I have to make poems for them. God knows how tired I am of using the insanity of Van Gogh and the adventures of Gauguin as can-openers for the ambitious Count Six-Times. And how sick I am of literary bitches. But they're the only kind that'll have me. . . . Listen, Balso, for a dollar I'll sell you a brief outline of my position."

Balso gave the dollar to get rid of him and received in return a little pamphlet.

THE PAMPHLET

Yesterday, while debating whether I should shave or not, news of the death of my friend Saniette arrived. I decided not to shave.

Today, while shaving, I searched myself for yesterday's

emotions. Searched, that is, the pockets of my dressing gown and the shelves of the medicine closet. Not finding anything, I looked further. I looked [first smiling, of course] into the bowels of my compassion, the depths of my being, and even into the receding vistas of my memory. I came from my search, as was to be expected, empty-handed. My "Open, oh flood gates of feeling! Empty, oh vials of passion!" made certain and immediate the defeat of my purpose.

That I failed in my search was for me a sign of my intelligence. I am [just as children choose sides to play "cops and robbers" or "Indians and cowboys"] on the side of intellect against the emotions, on the side of the brain against the heart. Nevertheless, I recognized the cardboard and tin of my position [a young man, while shaving, dismisses Death with a wave of his hand] and did not give up my search for an emotion. I marshalled all my reasons for grief [I had lived with Saniette for almost two years], yet failed to find sorrow.

Death is a very difficult thing for me to consider sincerely because I find certain precomposed judgments awaiting my method of consideration to render it absurd. No matter how I form my comment I attach to it the criticisms sentimental, satirical, formal. With these judgments there goes a series of literary associations which remove me still further from genuine feeling. The very act of recognizing Death, Love, Beauty—all the major subjects—has become, from literature and exercise, impossible.

After admitting to myself that I had failed, I tried to cover my defeat by practicing a few sneers in the bathroom mirror. I remembered that yesterday I had used Saniette's death as an excuse for not shaving and added in a loud voice, "Just as more than one friend will use the occasion of my death as an excuse for breaking an undesired appointment."

Heartened by my sneering reflection in the mirror, I pictured the death of Saniette. Hiding under the blankets of her hospital bed and invoking the aid of Mother Eddy and Doctor Coué: "I won't die! I am getting better and better. I won't die! The will is master o'er the flesh. I won't die!" Only to have Death answer: "Oh, yes you will." And she had. I made Death's triumph my own.

The inevitability of death has always given me pleasure, not because I am eager to die, but because all the Saniettes must die. When the preacher explained the one thing all men could be certain of—all must die—the King of France became angry. When death prevailed over the optimism of Saniette, she was, I am certain, surprised. The thought of Saniette's surprise pleases me, just as the King's anger must have pleased the preacher.

Only a portion of my dislike for Saniette is based on the natural antipathy pessimists feel for optimists, cowboys for Indians, cops for robbers. For a large part it consists of that equally natural antipathy felt by the performer for his audience. My relations with Saniette were exactly those of performer and audience.

While living with me, Saniette accepted my most desperate feats in somewhat the manner one watches the marvelous stunts of acrobats. Her casualness excited me so that I became more and more desperate in my performances. A tragedy with only one death is nothing in the theatre—why not two deaths? Why not a hundred? With some such idea as this in mind I exhibited my innermost organs: I wore my heart and genitals around my neck. At each exhibition I watched carefully to see how she received my performance—with a smile or with a tear.

Though I exhibited myself as a clown, I wanted no mistakes to be made; I was a tragic clown.

I have forgotten the time when I could look back at an affair with a woman and remember anything but a sequence of theatrical poses—poses that I assumed, no matter how aware I was of their ridiculousness, because they were amusing. All my acting has but one purpose, the attraction of the female.

If it had been possible for me to attract by exhibiting a series of physical charms, my hatred would have been less. But I found it necessary to substitute strange conceits, wise and witty sayings, peculiar conduct, Art, for the muscles, teeth, hair, of my rivals.

All this much-exhibited intelligence is but a development of the instinct to please. My case is similar to that of a bird called the Amblyornis inornata. As his name indicates, the Inornata is a dull-colored, ugly bird. Yet the Inornata is cousin to the Bird of Paradise. Because he lacks his cousin's brilliant plumage, he has to exteriorize internal feathers. The Inornata plants a garden and builds a house of flowers as a substitute for the gay feathers of his relative. Of course the female Inornata loves her shabby artist dearly; yet when a friend passes, Mrs. Bird of Paradise can say, "Show your tail, dear," while Mrs. Inornata, to her confusion, has no explanation to give for her love. If she is in a temper she might even ask Mr. Inornata to exteriorize a few internal feathers. Still more, the Bird of Paradise cannot be blamed for the quality of his tail—it just grew. The Inornata, however, is held personally responsible for his performance as an artist.

There was a time when I felt that I was indeed a rare spirit. Then I had genuinely expressed my personality with a babe's delight in confessing the details of its inner life. Soon, however, in order to interest my listeners, I found it necessary to shorten my long outpourings; to make them, by straining my imagination, spectacular. Oh, how much work goes into the search for the odd, the escape from the same!

Because of women like Saniette, I acquired the habit of extravagant thought. I now convert everything into fantastic entertainment and the extraordinary has become an obsession. . . .

An intelligent man finds it easy to laugh at himself, but his laughter is not sincere if it is thorough. If I could be Hamlet, or even a clown with a breaking heart 'neath his jester's motley, the role would be tolerable. But I always find it necessary to burlesque the mystery of feeling at its source; I must laugh at myself, and if the laugh is "bitter," I must laugh at the laugh. The ritual of feeling demands burlesque and, whether the burlesque is successful or not, a laugh. . . .

One night, while in a hotel bedroom with Saniette, I grew miserably sick of the mad dreams I had been describing to amuse her. I began to beat her. While beating her, I was unable to forget that strange man, John Raskolnikov Gilson, the Russian student. As I beat her, I shouted: "O constipation of desire! O diarrhoea of love! O life within life! O mystery of being! O Young Women's Christian Association! Oh! Oh!"

When her screams brought the hotel clerk to our door, I attempted to explain my irritation. In part I said: "This evening I am very nervous. I have a sty on my eye, a cold sore on my lip, a pimple where the edge of my collar touches my neck, another pimple in the corner of my mouth, and a drop of salt snot on the end of my nose. Because I rub them continually my nostrils are inflamed, sore and angry.

"My forehead is wrinkled so hard that it hurts, yet I cannot unwrinkle it. I spend many hours trying to unwrinkle my forehead. I try to catch myself by surprise; I try to smooth my forehead with my fingers; I try to concentrate my whole mind to this end, but I am unable to make smooth my brow. The skin over my eyebrows is tied in an aching, unbreakable knot.

"The wood of this table, the glasses on it, this girl's woollen dress, the skin under it, excites and annoys me. It seems to me as though all the materials of life—wood, glass, wool, skin—are rubbing against my sty, my cold sore and my pimples; rubbing in such a way as not to satisfy the itch or convert irritation into active pain, but so as to increase the size of the irritation, magnify it and make it seem to cover everything—hysteria, despair.

"I go to a mirror and squeeze the sty with all my strength. I tear off the cold sore with my nails. I scrub my salt-encrusted nostrils with the rough sleeve of my overcoat. If I could only turn irritation into pain; could push the whole thing into insanity and so escape. I am able to turn irritation into active pain for only a few seconds, but the pain soon subsides and the monotonous rhythm of irritation returns. O how fleeting is pain!—I cry. I think of sandpapering my body. I think of grease, of sandalwood oil, of saliva; I think of velvet, of Keats, of music, of the hardness of precious stones, of mathematics, of the arrangements of architecture. But, alas! I can find no relief."

Both Saniette and the clerk refused to understand. Saniette said that she understood the irritation I was talking about was one of the spirit; yet, she added, the only conclusion she could arrive at—a gentleman would never strike a lady—was that I no longer loved her. The clerk murmured something about the police.

In order to get him away from the door, I asked him if he had ever heard of the Marquis de Sade or of Gilles de Rais. Fortunately, we were in a Broadway hotel whose employees are familiar with the world. When I mentioned these names, the clerk bowed and left us with a smile. Saniette was also of the world; she smiled and went back to bed.

The next morning, remembering their smiles, I thought it advisable to explain my actions again. Not that it was necessary for me to differentiate between the kind of a beating alcohol inspires a temperance-cartoon drunkard to give his hard-working spouse, and the beating I had given Saniette; but, rather, that I found it difficult to illustrate the point I desired to make clear.

"When you think of me, Saniette," I said, "think of two men—myself and the chauffeur within me. This chauffeur is very large and dressed in ugly ready-made clothing. His shoes, soiled from walking about the streets of a great city, are covered with animal ordure and chewing gum. His hands are covered with coarse woollen gloves. On his head is a derby hat.

"The name of this chauffeur is The Desire to Procreate.

"He sits within me like a man in an automobile. His heels are in my bowels, his knees on my heart, his face in my brain. His gloved hands hold me firmly by the tongue; his hands, covered with wool, refuse me speech for the emotions aroused by the face in my brain.

"From within, he governs the sensations I receive through my fingers, eyes, tongue and ears.

"Can you imagine how it feels to have this cloth-covered devil within one? While naked, were you ever embraced by a fully clothed man? Do you remember how his button-covered coat felt, how his heavy shoes felt against your skin? Imagine having this man inside of you, fumbling and fingering your heart and tongue with wool-covered hands, treading your tender organs with stumbling soiled feet."

Because of the phrasing of my complaint, Saniette was able to turn my revenge into a joke. She weathered a second beating with a slow, kind smile.

Saniette represents a distinct type of audience—smart, sophisticated, sensitive yet hardboiled, art-loving frequenters of the little theatres. I am their particular kind of a performer.

Some day I shall obtain my revenge by writing a play for one of their art theatres. A theatre patronized by the discriminating few: art-lovers and book-lovers, school teachers who adore the grass-eating Shaw, sensitive young Jews who adore culture, lending librarians, publisher's assistants, homosexualists and homosexualists' assistants, hard-drinking newspaper men, interior decorators, and the writers of advertising copy.

In this play I shall take my beloved patrons into my confidence and flatter their difference from other theatre-goers. I shall congratulate them on their good taste in preferring Art to animal acts. Then, suddenly, in the midst of some very witty dialogue, the entire cast will walk to the footlights and shout Chekov's advice:

"It would be more profitable for the farmer to raise rats for the granary than for the bourgeois to nourish the artist, who must always be occupied with undermining institutions."

In case the audience should misunderstand and align itself on the side of the artist, the ceiling of the theatre will be made to open and cover the occupants with tons of loose excrement. After the deluge, if they so desire, the patrons of my art can gather in the customary charming groups and discuss the play.

✿

When he had finished reading, Balso threw the pamphlet away with a sigh. In his childhood, things had been managed differently; besides, shaving had not been permitted before the age of sixteen. Having no alternative, Balso blamed the war, the invention of printing, nineteenth-century science, communism, the wearing of soft hats, the use of contraceptives, the large number of delicatessen stores, the movies, the tabloids, the lack of adequate ventilation in large cities, the passing of the saloon, the soft collar fad, the spread of foreign art, the decline of the western world, commercialism, and, finally, for throwing the artist back on his own personality, the renaissance.

"What is beauty saith my sufferings then?" asked Balso of himself, quoting Marlowe.

As though in answer to his question, he saw standing naked before him a slim young girl busily washing her hidden charms in a public fountain. Through the wood of his brain there buzzed the saw of desire.

She called to him, saying:

"Charge, oh poet, the red-veined flowers of suddenly remembered intimacies—the foliage of memory. Feel, oh poet, the warm knife of thought swift stride and slit in the ready garden.

"Soon the hot seed will come to thwart the knife's progress. The hot seed will come in a joyous burst-birth of reeking undergrowth and swamp forest.

"Walk toward the houses of the city of your memory, oh poet! Houses that are protuberances on the skin of streets—warts, tumors, pimples, corns, nipples, sebaceous cysts, hard and soft chancres.

"Like the gums of false teeth, red are the signs imploring you to enter the game paths lit by iron flowers. Like ants under a new-turned stone, hysterical are the women who run there clad in the silk tights of pleasure, oiled with

fish slime. Women whose only delight is to rub the jaded
until it becomes irritated and grows new things, pimples of
a . . ."

Throwing his arms around her, Balso interrupted her
recitation by sticking his tongue into her mouth. But when
he closed his eyes to heighten the fun, he felt that he was
embracing tweed. He opened them and saw that what he
held in his arms was a middle aged woman dressed in a
mannish suit and wearing hornrimmed glasses.

"My name is Miss McGeeney," she said. "I am a writer
as well as a school teacher. Let's discuss something."

Balso wanted to bash her jaw in, but he found that he
could not move. He tried to curse, but could only say:
"How interesting. On what are you working?"

"At present I am writing a biography of Samuel Perkins.
Stark, clever, disillusioned stuff, with a tenderness devoid
of sentiment, yet touched by pity and laughter and irony.
Into this book I hope to put the whimsical humor, the
kindly satire of a mellow life.

"On the surface *Samuel Perkins: Smeller* [for so I call it]
is simply a delightful story for children. The discriminating
adult soon discovers, however, that it sprang from the
brain of a kindly philosopher, that it is a genial satire on
humanity.

"Under the title I intend placing as motto a verse from
Juvenal: 'Who is surprised to see a goiter in the Alps? Quis
tumidum guttur miratur in Alpibus?' I feel that this quota-
tion strikes the keynote of the work.

"But who is Samuel Perkins, you are probably wonder-
ing. Samuel Perkins is the biographer of E. F. Fitzgerald.
And who is Fitzgerald? You are of course familiar with
D. B. Hobson's life of Boswell. Well, E. F. Fitzgerald is the
author of a life of Hobson. The subject of my biography,
Samuel Perkins, wrote a life of Fitzgerald.

"Sometime ago, a publisher asked me to write a biography, and I decided to do one of E. F. Fitzgerald. Fortunately, before commencing my study, I met Samuel Perkins who told me that he had written a biography of Fitzgerald the biographer of Hobson the biographer of Boswell. This news did not discourage me, but, on the contrary, made me determine to write a life of Perkins and so become another link in a brilliant literary chain. It seems to me that someone must surely take the hint and write the life of Miss McGeeney, the woman who wrote the biography of the man who wrote the biography of the man who wrote the biography of the man who wrote the biography of Boswell. And that, ad infinitum, we will all go rattling down the halls of time, each one in his or her turn a tin can on the tail of Doctor Johnson.

"But there are other good reasons for writing a life of Perkins. He was a great, if peculiar, genius with a character that lends itself most readily to biography.

"At an age when most men's features are regular, before his personality had been able to elevate any one portion of his physiognomy over the rest, Perkins' face was dominated by his nose. This fact I have ascertained from a collection of early photographs lent me by a profound admirer of Perkins and a fellow practitioner of his art. I refer to Robert Jones, author of a book called *Nosologie*.

"When I met Perkins for the first time, his face reminded me of the body of a man I had known at college. According to gossip current in the girls' dormitory this man abused himself. The source of these rumors lay in the peculiar shape of his body: all the veins, muscles and sinews flowed toward and converged at one point. In a like manner the wrinkles on Perkins' face, the contours of his head, the lines of his brow and chin, seemed to have melted and run into his nose.

"At this first meeting, Perkins said something that was later to prove very illuminating. He quoted Lucretius to the effect that 'his nose was quicker to scent a fetid sore or a rank armpit, than a dog to smell out the hidden sow.' Like most quotations, this one is only partially true. True, that is, of only one stage in Perkins' aesthetic development—the, what I have called quite arbitrarily, excrement period.

"It is possible to explain the powers of Perkins' magnificent sense of smell by the well-known theory of natural compensation. No one who has ever observed the acuteness of touch exhibited by a blind man or the gigantic shoulders of a legless man, will question the fact that Nature compensates for the loss of one attribute by lavishing her bounty on another. And Nature had made in the person of Samuel Perkins another attempt at justice. He was deaf and almost blind; his fingers fumbled stupidly; his mouth was always dry and contained a dull, insensitive tongue. But his nose! His nose was a marvelously sensitive and nice instrument. Nature had concentrated in his sense of smell all the abilities usually distributed among the five senses. She had strengthened this organ and had made it so sensitive that it was able to do duty for all the contact organs. Perkins was able to translate the sensations, sound, sight, taste, and touch, into that of smell. He could smell a chord in D minor, or distinguish between the tone-smell of a violin and that of a viola. He could smell the caress of velvet and the strength of iron. It has been said of him that he could smell an isosceles triangle; I mean that he could apprehend through the sense of smell the principles involved in isosceles triangles.

"In the ability to interpret the functions of one sense in terms of another, he is not alone. A French poet, in a sonnet of the vowels, called the letter I red and the letter U blue. Another symbolist, Father Castel, made a clavichord on which he was able to play melody and harmony by using color. Des Esseintes, Huysmans' hero, used a taste organ on which he composed symphonies for the palate.

"But can you imagine, new-found friend and esteemed poet, how horrible was the predicament of this sensitive and sensuous man forced to interpret the whole external world through conclusions reached by the sense of smell alone? If we have great difficulty in discovering the Real, how much greater must his difficulty have been?

"In my presence, Perkins once called the senses a tread-mill. 'A tread-mill,' he said, 'on which one can go only from the odors of Indian-grass baskets to the sour smells of Africa and the stink of decay.'

"Rather than a tread-mill, I should call the senses a circle. A step forward along the circumference of a circle is a step nearer the starting place. Perkins went, along the circumference of the circle of his senses, from anticipation to realization, from hunger to satiation, from naïveté to sophistication, from simplicity to perversion. He went [speaking in Perkinsesque] from the smell of new-mown hay to that of musk and vervain [from the primitive to the romantic], and from vervain to sweat and excrement [from the romantic to the realistic]; and, finally, to complete the circuit, from excrement he returned to new-mown hay.

"There is, however, a way out for the artist and Perkins discovered it. The circumference of a circle infinite in size is a straight line. And a man like Perkins is able to make the circle of his sensory experience approach the infinite. He can so qualify the step from simplicity to perversion, for example, that the curve which makes inevitable the return to simplicity is imperceptible.

"One day Perkins told me that he was going to be married. I asked him if he thought his wife would understand him, and whether he thought he could be happy with a woman. He answered no to both questions, and said that he was marrying as an artist. I asked him to explain. He replied that the man who had numbered the smells of the human body and found them to be seven was a fool, unless the number was used in its mystic sense.

"After studying this strange conversation with the master, I discovered his meaning. He had found in the odors of a woman's body, never-ending, ever-fresh variation and change—a world of dreams, seas, roads, forests, textures, colors, flavors, forms. On my questioning him further, he confirmed my interpretation. He told me that he had built from the odors of his wife's body an architecture and an aesthetic, a music and a mathematic. Counterpoint, multiplication, the square of a sensation, the cube root of an experience—all were there. He told me that he had even discovered a politic, a hierarchy of odors: self-government, direct . . ."

By this time, Balso had gotten one of his hands free. He hit Miss McGeeney a terrific blow in the gut and hove her into the fountain.

The wooden horse, Balso realized as he walked on, was inhabited solely by writers in search of an audience, and he was determined not to be tricked into listening to another story. If one had to be told, he would tell it.

As he hurried down the seemingly endless corridor, he began to wonder whether he would ever reach the Anus Mirabilis again. His feet hurt badly and his head ached. When he came to a café built into the side of the intestine, he sat down and ordered a glass of beer. After drinking the beer, he took a newspaper out of his pocket, put it over his face and went to sleep.

Balso dreamt that he was a young man again, lurking in a corner of the Carnegie Hall lobby among the assembled friends and relatives of music. The lobby was crowded with the many beautiful girl-cripples who congregate there because Art is their only solace, most men looking upon their strange forms with distaste. But it was otherwise with Balso Snell. He likened their disarranged hips, their short legs, their humps, their splay feet, their wall-eyes, to ornament. Their strange foreshortenings, hanging heads, bulging spinesacks, were a delight, for he had ever preferred the imperfect, knowing well the plainness, the niceness of perfection.

Spying a beautiful hunchback, he suddenly became sick with passion. The cripple of his choice looked like some creature from the depths of the sea. She was tall and extraordinarily hunched. She was tall in spite of her enormous hump; but for her dog-leg spine she would have been seven feet high. Moreover, he could be certain that, like all hunchbacks, she was intelligent.

He tipped his hat to her. She smiled and he snatched her from the throng, crying as he took her arm:

"O arabesque, I, Balso Snell, shall replace music in your affections! Your pleasures shall no longer be vicarious. No longer shall you mentally pollute yourself. For me, your sores are like flowers: the new, pink, budlike sores, the full, rose-ripe sores, the sweet, seed-bearing sores. I shall cherish them all. O deviation from the Golden Mean! O out of alignment!"

The Lepi [for so did he instantly dub her] opened her mouth to reply and exhibited one hundred and forty-four exquisite teeth in rows of four.

"Balso," she said, "you are a villain. Do you love as do all villains?"

"No," he answered, "I love only this." As he spoke, he laid his cool white hands upon her beautiful, hydrocephalic forehead. Then, bending over her enormous hump, he kissed her full on the brow.

Feeling his lips on her forehead, Janey Davenport, [the Lepi] gazed out over the blue waves of the Mediterranean and felt the delight of being young, rich, beautiful. No-one had ever before forgotten her strange shape long enough to realize how beautiful her soul was. She had never before known the thrill of being subdued by a male from a different land from that of her dreams. Now she had found a wonderful poet; now she knew the thrill she had never known before . . . had found it in the strength of this young and tall, strangely wise man, caught like herself in the meshes of the greatest net human hearts can know: Love.

Balso took her home and, in the hallway of her house, tried to seduce her. She allowed him one kiss, then broke away. From her lips—overhung by a moist eye and underhung by a heaving embonpoint—there came, "Love is a strange thing, is it not, Balso Snell?" He was afraid to laugh; he knew that if he even smiled the jig would be up. "Love," she said, "is beautiful. You, Balso, do not love. Love is sacred. How can you kiss if you do not love?" When he began to unbutton, she said with a desperately gay smile: "Would you want some one to ask of your sister what you ask of me? So this is why you invited me to dinner? I prefer music."

He made another attempt, but she fended him off. "Love," she began again, "Love, with me, Mr. Snell, is sacred. I shall never debase love, or myself, or the memory of my mother, in a hallway. Act your education, Mr.

Snell. Tumbling in hallways at my age! How can you? After all, there are the eternal verities, not to speak of the janitor. And besides, we were never properly introduced."

After half an hour's sparring, he managed to warm her up a bit. She held him to her tightly for a second, capsized her eyeballs, and said: "If you only loved me, Balso. If you only loved me." He looked her in the eye, stroked her hump, kissed her brow, protesting desperately: "But I do love you, Janey. I do. I do. I swear it. I must have you. I must! I must!" She shoved him away with a sad yet determined smile. "First you will have to prove your love as did the knights of old."

"I'm ready," Balso cried. "What would you have me do?"

"Come inside and I'll tell you."

Balso followed her into the apartment and sat down beside her on a couch.

"I want you to kill a man called Beagle Darwin," she said with great firmness. "He betrayed me. In this hump on my back I carry his child. After you have killed him, I shall yield up my pink and white body to you, and then commit suicide."

"A bargain," Balso said. "Give me but your stocking to wear around my hat and I'm off to earn the prize."

"Not so fast, my gallant; first I must explain a few things to you.

"After listening to Beagle Darwin recite some of his poetry, I slept with him one night while my folks were visiting friends in Plainfield, New Jersey. Unfamiliar as I was with the wiles of men, I believed him when he told me that he loved me and wanted to take me to Paris to live in an artistic studio. I was very happy until I received the following letter."

Here the Lepi went to a bureau and took out two letters, one of which she gave Balso to read.

Darling Janey:

You persist in misunderstanding me. Please understand this: It is for your own good that I am refusing to take you to Paris, as I am firmly convinced that such a trip can only result in your death.

Here is the way in which you would die:

In your pajamas, Janey, you sit near the window and listen to the gay clatter of Paris traffic. The highpitched automobile horns make of every day a holiday. You are miserable.

You tell yourself: Oh, the carnival crowds are always hurrying past my window. I'm like an old actor mumbling Macbeth as he fumbles in the garbage can outside the theatre of his past triumphs. Only I'm not old; I'm young. Young, and I never had any triumphs to mumble over; my only triumphs were those I dreamed of having. I'm Janey Davenport, pregnant, unmarried, unloved, lonely, watching the laughing crowds hurry past her window.

I don't fit into life. I don't fit into his life. He only tolerates me for my body. He only wants one thing from me, and I want, oh how I want, love.

The ridiculous, the ridiculous, all day long he talks of nothing else but how ridiculous this, that, or the other thing is. And he means me. I am absurd. He is never satisfied with calling other people ridiculous, with him everything is ridiculous—himself, me. Of course I can laugh at Mother with him, or at the Hearth; but why must my own mother and home be ridiculous? I can laugh at Hobey, Joan, but I don't want to laugh at myself. I'm tired of laugh, laugh, laugh. I want to retain some portion of myself unlaughed at. There is something in me that I won't laugh at. I won't. I'll laugh at the outside world all he wants me to, but I won't, I don't want to laugh at my inner world. It's all right for him to say: "Be hard! Be an intellectual! Think, don't feel!" But I want to be soft. I want to feel. I don't want to think. I feel blue when I think. I want to keep a hard, outside surface towards the world, and a soft, inner side for him. And I want him to do the same, so that we can be secure in each other's love. But with his rotten, ugly jokes he keeps me at arm's length just when I want to be confiding and tender. When I show him my soft side he laughs. I don't want to be always on my guard against his laughter. There are times when I want to put down my armor. I am tired of eternally bearing armor against the world. Love is a merging, not an occasion for intellectual warfare. I want to enjoy my emotions. I want, sometimes, to play the child, and to make love like a child—tenderly, confidingly, prettily. I'm sick of his taunts.

Pregnant, unmarried, and he won't marry me. If I ask him to, he will laugh his terrible horse-laugh: "Well, my little bohemian, you want to get out of it, do you? Life, however, is Life; and the Realities are the Realities. You can't have your cake and eat it too, you know." He'll tell his friends the story as a joke—one of his unexplainable jokes. All his smug-faced friends will laugh at me, especially the Paige girl.

They don't like me; I don't fit in. All my life I have been a misfit—misunderstood. The carnival crowds are always hurrying past my window. As a kid, I never liked to play in the streets with the other kids; I always wanted to stay in the house and read a book. Since my father's death, I have no one to go to with my misery. He was always willing to understand and comfort me. Oh, how I want to be understood by someone who really loves me. Mother, like Beagle, always laughs at me. If they want to be kind it is, "You silly goose!" If they are angry, "Don't be an idiot."

Only father was sympathetic, and he is dead. I wish I were dead.

Joan Higgins would know what to do if she were in my position—pregnant and unmarried. Joan fits into the kind of a life he and his friends lead better than I do. Like the time Joan said she had gone back to live with Hobey because it was such a bore looking for healthy men to sleep with. Joan warned me against him; she said he wasn't my kind. I thought him just my kind, sad and a poet. He is sad, but with a nasty sadness—all jeers for his own sadness. "It's the war. Everybody is sad nowadays. Great stuff, pessimism." Still he is sad; if he would only stop acting we could be very happy together. I want so much to comfort him—mother him.

Joan's advice would probably be for me to make him marry me. How he would howl. "Make an honest girl of you, eh?"

You can see the Café Carcas from the window. You are living in the Rue de la Grande Chaumiere, at the Hotel Liberia.

Why don't I fit in well at the Carcas? Joan would go big there. Why don't they like me? I'm as good looking as she is, and as clever. It's because I don't let myself go the way she does. Well, I don't want to. There is something fine in me that won't let me degrade myself.

You see me come out of the café, laughing and waving my arms.

I hope he comes upstairs.

You see me turn, and come towards the hotel.

Just as soon as he comes in I'll tell him I'm pregnant. I'll tell him in a matter-of-fact voice—casually. As long as I keep my tone casual he won't be able to laugh.

"Hello darling, how are you this morning?"
"All right. Beagle, je suis enceinte."
"You're what?"
[Oh, damn my pronunciation, I spoilt it.] "I'm pregnant." Despite your desire to appear casual you let a note of heartbreak into your voice. You droop.

"We'll have a party tonight and celebrate." I leave the room, shutting the door behind me, carefully.

Perhaps he'll never come back . . . You run to the window—sick. You sit down and prepare to indulge your misery. Your misery, your misery—you roll, you grovel in it. I'm pregnant! I'm pregnant! I'm pregnant! You force the rhythm of this cry into your blood. After the first moments of hysterical anguish are over, you wrap your predicament around you, snuggling into it, letting it cover you completely like a blanket. Your big trouble shelters you from a host of minor troubles. You are so miserable.

You remember that "life is a prison without bars," and think of suicide.

No one ever listens to me when I talk of suicide. The night I woke up in bed with him, it was no different. He thought I was joking when I said that I had frightened myself by brooding on death. But I told the truth. Death and suicide are never far from my thoughts. I said that death is like putting on a wet bathing suit. Now death seems warm and friendly. No, death is still like putting on a wet suit—shivery.

If I do it, I won't leave a note behind for him to laugh at. Just end it, that's all. No matter how I word a farewell note he will find something to laugh at—something to show his friends as a joke . . .

Mother knows I'm living with a man in Paris. Sophie wrote that everybody is talking about me. If I were to go home—even if I were not pregnant—mother would make an awful stink. I don't want to go back to the States: a long dull trip followed by a long dull life teaching elementary school.

What can I expect from him? He'll want me to have an abortion. They say that on account of the decreasing birth rate it is hard to get a competent doctor to do the operation. The French police are very strict. If the doctor killed me . . .

If I kill myself, I kill my body. I don't want to destroy my body; it is a good body—soft, white, and kind to me—a beautiful, happy body. If he were a true poet he would love me for my body's beauty; but he is like all men; he wants only one thing. Soon my body will be swollen and clumsy. The milk spoils the shape of a woman's breasts after an abortion. When my body becomes ugly, he will hate me. I once hoped that having a child would draw him closer to me—make him love me as a mother. But mother for him is always Mammy: a popular Broadway ballad, Mammy, Mammy, my old Kentucky Home, put it all together, it spells Mother. He doesn't see that Mother can mean shelter, love, intimacy. Oh, how much I want, I need, love.

If I wanted to make a squawk, mother would force him to marry me; but she would scold terribly and make a horrible scene. I'm too tired and sick to go through with a shotgun wedding.

Maybe I passed my period because of the wine—no, I know. Where did I read, "In my belly there is a tangled forest of arms and legs." It sounds like his stuff. When he left, he said he'd give a party tonight in honor of the occasion. I know what kind of a party it will be. He'll get drunk and make a speech: "Big with child, great with young—let me toast your gut, my dear. Here's to the pup! Waiters, stand erect while I toast my heir." He and his friends will expect me to join in the sport—to be a good sport.

He claims that the only place to commit suicide is on Chekov's grave. The Seine is also famous for suicide: "'midst the bustle of 'Gay Paree'—suicide." "She killed herself in Paris." There is something tragic in the very thought. French windows make it easy; all you have to do is open the window and walk out. Every window over the third floor is a door into heaven. When I arrive there I can plead my belly—oh, how bitterly cruel the jest is. "Jest?" He would correct me—"not 'jest,' my dear, but joke; never, never say 'jest.'"

Oh, how miserable I am. I need love; I can't live without someone to treasure and comfort me. If I jumped from the third floor I might cripple myself—lucky this room is on the fourth. Lucky? [Animals never commit suicide.]

And mother—what would mother say? Mother would feel worse about my being unmarried than about my death. I could leave a note asking him, as a final favor, to write her and say that we were married. He would forget to write.

When I'm dead, I'll be out of it all. Mother, Beagle—they will leave me alone. But I can't blame my trouble on him. I got myself into this mess. I went to his room after he acted decently in mine. I was jealous of Joan; she had so much fun going to men's rooms, and all that sort of thing. How childish Joan and her follies seem to me now.

When I'm dead the whole world as far as I am concerned—Beagle, mother—will be dead also. Or aussi: I came to Paris to learn French. I certainly learnt French. I wasn't even able to tell him in French without turning my trouble into a joke.

What love and a child by the man I loved once meant to

me—and to live in Paris. If he should come back suddenly and catch me like this, brooding at the window, he'd say:
"A good chance for you to kill two birds with one stone, my
dear; but remember, an egg in the belly is worth more than
a bird in the bush." What a pig he is! He thinks I haven't
the nerve to kill myself. He patronizes me as though I were
a child. "Suicide," he says, "is a charming affectation on the
part of a young Russian, but in you, dear Janey, it is
absurd."

You scream with irritation: "I'm serious! I am! I am! I
don't want to live! I'm miserable! I don't want to live!"

I'm only teasing myself with thoughts of suicide at an
open window. I know I won't do it. Mother will call me
away: "Go away from that window—fool! You'll catch your
death-cold or fall out—clumsy!"

At the word "clumsy" you fall to your death in the gut-
ter below the window.

Horrible, eh? Yes, Janey, it is a suicide's grave that I
saved you from when I refused to take you to Paris.

Yours,

Beagle

When Balso had finished reading, she handed him the
other letter.

Darling Janey:

You did not take offence, I hope, at my letter. Please
believe me when I say that I tried to make my treatment
of your suicide as impersonal as possible. I did my best
to keep the description of both our characters scientific
and just. If I treated you savagely, I treated myself no
gentler. It is true that I concentrated on you, but only
because it was your suicide. In this letter I shall try to

show, and so even the score, how I would have received your death.

You once said to me that I talk like a man in a book. I not only talk, but think and feel like one. I have spent my life in books; literature has deeply dyed my brain its own color. This literary coloring is a protective one—like the brown of the rabbit or the checks of the quail—making it impossible for me to tell where literature ends and I begin.

I start where I left off in my last letter:

As Janey's half-naked body crashed into the street, the usual crowds were hurrying to lunch from the Academies Colorossa and Grande Chaumiere; the concierge was coming out of the hotel's side door. In order to avoid running over her body, the driver of a cab coming from the Rue Notre Dame des Champs and going toward the Square de la Grande Chaumiere, brought his machine to a stop with screaming brakes. The concierge, on seeing the cab stop suddenly, one wheel over the body of a tenant of his, ran up, caught the chauffeur by the arm, and called loudly for the police. No one had seen her fall but the driver of the cab; he, bursting with rage, called the concierge an idiot, and pointed to the open window from which she had jumped. A crowd gathered around the chauffeur and shouted at him angrily. A policeman arrived. He, too, refused to believe the cab-driver, although he noticed that the dead girl was in her pajamas. "What would she be doing in the street in her night-clothes if she hadn't fallen from the window?" He shrugged his shoulders: "These American art students."

Beagle, on his way to the Café Carcas for a drink, turned to see where so many people were running. He saw the gesticulating group around the cab and went back, grateful for any diversion on what had been such a dull morning. As he joined them he kept thinking of Janey's announcement. "I'm pregnant." It reminded him of another announcement of hers. "It's about time I took a lover." "I'm pregnant" demanded for an answer, Life, just as "It's about time I took a lover" had been worthy of no less a reply than Love. She made a habit of these startling declarations: a few words, but freighted with meaning.

He knew what "I'm pregnant" meant; it meant canvassing his friends for the whereabouts of a doctor willing to perform the operation and writing frantic letters to the States for the necessary money. Through it all, Janey, having thrown the responsibility on him, would sit in one corner of the room: "Do with me what you will"—the groaning, patient, all-suffering, all-knowing, what has to be will be, beast of many burdens.

As he pushed into the crowd, someone told him a girl had been killed. He looked where the chauffeur was pointing and saw the open window of their room. Then he saw Janey under the cab; he could not see her face, but he recognized her pajamas.

This was indeed a solution. The problem had been solved for him with a vengeance. He turned away and hurried up the street, afraid of being recognized. It had become impossible for him to take his drink at the Carcas. If he went there some friend would surely come to him with the news: "Beagle! Beagle! Janey has killed herself." He wanted to go somewhere and prepare a reply. "Here today and gone tomorrow" would never do, even at the Carcas.

He went past the Carcas up the Rue Delambre to the Avenue de Maine. On this street he went into a café hardly ever visited by Americans and sat down at a table in the corner of an inside room. He called for some cognac and asked himself:

Of what assistance could I have been? Should I have gone down on my knees in the street and wept over her dead body? Torn my hair? Called on the Deity? Or should I have gone calmly up to the policeman and said: "I'm her husband. Allow me to accompany you to the morgue."

He ordered another cognac—Beagle Darwin the Destroyer. He pulled his hat down over his eyes and tossed off his drink.

She did it because she was pregnant. I would have married her, the fool. I hurt her when I made believe I didn't understand her French. "Je suis enceinte." My "what" was one of the astonishment, not the "what" of interrogation. No, it was not. You said "what" in order to humiliate her. What is the purpose of all your harping on petty affectations? Why this continual irritation at the sight of other peoples' stupidities? What of your own stupidities and affectations? Why is it impossible for you to understand, except in terms of art, her action? She killed herself because she was afraid to face her troubles—an abortion or the birth of a bastard. Absurd; she never asked you to marry her. You do not understand.

He crouched over his drink, Tiger Darwin, his eyes half shut—desperate.

I wonder if she was able to avoid generalizing before she killed herself. I am sure it was not trouble, that was uppermost in her mind, but the rag-tag of some "philosophy." Although I did my best to laugh away finita la comedia, I am certain that some such catch-word of disillusion was in her mouth when she turned the trick. She probably decided that Love, Life, Death, all could be contained in an epigram: "The things which are of value in Life are empty and rotten and trifling; Love is but a flitting shadow, a lure, a gimcrack, a kickshaw. And Death?—bah! What, then, is there still detaining you in this vale of tears?" Can it be that the only thing that bothers me in a statement of this sort is the wording? Or it is because there is something arty about suicide? Suicide: Werther, the Cosmic Urge, the Soul, the Quest, and Otto Greenbaum, Phil Beta Kappa, Age seventeen—Life is unworthy of him; and Haldington Knape, Oxford, author, man-about-town, big game hunter—Life is too tiresome; and Terry Kornflower, poet, no hat, shirt open to the navel—Life is too crude; and Janey Davenport, pregnant, unmarried, jumps from a studio window in Paris—Life is too difficult. O. Greenbaum, H. Knape, T. Kornflower, J. Davenport, all would agree that "Life is but the span from womb to tomb; a sigh, a smile; a chill, a fever; a throe of pain, a spasm of volupty: then a gasping for breath, and the comedy is over, the song is ended, ring down the curtain, the clown is dead."

The clown is dead; the curtain is down. And when I say clown, I mean you. After all, aren't we all . . . aren't we all clowns? Of course, I know it's old stuff; but what difference does that make? Life *is* a stage; and *we* are clowns. What is more tragic than the role of clown? What more filled with all the essentials of great art?—pity and irony. Get it? The thousands of sweating, laughing, grimacing, jeering animals out front—you have just set them in the aisles, when in comes a messenger. Your wife has run away with the boarder, your son has killed a man, the baby has cancer. Or maybe you ain't married. Coming from the bathroom, you discover that you have gonorrhoea, or you get a telegram that your mother is dead, or your father, or your sister, or your brother. Now get the picture. Outside, after your turn, the customers are hollering and screaming: "Do your stuff, kid! We want Beagle! Let's have Beagle! He's a wow!" The clowns down front are laughing, whistling, belching, crying, sweating, and eating peanuts. And you—you are back-stage, hiding in the shadow of an old prop. Clutching your bursting head with both hands, you hear nothing but the dull roar of your misfortunes. Slowly there filters through your clenched fingers the cries of your brother clowns. Your first thought is to rush out there and cut your throat before their faces with a last terrific laugh. But soon you are out front again doing your stuff, the same superb Beagle: dancing, laughing, singing—*acting*. Finally the curtain comes down, and, in your dressing room before the mirror, you make the faces that won't come off with the grease paint—the faces you will never make down front.

Beagle ordered another cognac and washed it down with a small beer. The saucers had begun to pile up before him on the table.

Well, Janey's death is a joke. A young, unmarried woman on discovering herself to be pregnant commits suicide. A very old and well-known way out of a very old and stale predicament. The moth and the candle, the fly and the spider, the butterfly and the rain, the clown and the curtain, all could be cited as having prepared one [oh how tediously!] for her suicide.

Another cognac! After this cognac, he would go to the Café Carcas and wait for a friend to bring him news of Janey's death.

How shall I receive the devastating news? In order to arouse no adverse criticism, it will be necessary for me to bear in mind that I come of an English-speaking race and therefore am cold, calm, collected, almost stolid, in the face of calamity. And, as the death is that of a very intimate friend, it is important that I show, in some subtle way, that I am hard hit for all my pretence of coldness. Or perhaps because the Carcas is full of artists, I can refuse to stop dreaming, refuse to leave my ivory tower, refuse to disturb that brooding white bird, my spirit. A wave of the hand:

"Yes, really. You don't say so?—quite dead." Or I can play one of my favorite roles, be the "Buffoon of the New Eternities" and cry: "Death, what is it? Life, what is it? Life is of course the absence of Death; and Death merely the absence of Life." But I might get into an argument unbecoming one who is lamenting the loss of a loved one. For the sake of the waiters, I will be a quiet, sober, gentle, umbrella-carrying Mr. B. Darwin, and out of a great sadness sob: "Oh, my darling, why did you do it? Oh why?" Or, best of all, like Hamlet, I will feign madness; for if they discover what lies in my heart they will lynch me.

MESSENGER
"Beagle! Beagle! Janey has fallen from the window and is no more."

PATRONS, WAITERS, ETC., AT THE CAFÉ CARCAS
"The girl you lived with is dead."
"Poor Janey. Poor Beagle. Terrible, terrible death."
"And so young she was, and so beautiful . . . in the cold street she lay."

B. HAMLET DARWIN
"Bromius! Iacchus! Son of Zeus!"

PATRONS, WAITERS, ETC.
"Don't you understand, man? The girl you lived with is dead. Your sweetheart is dead. She has killed herself. She is dead!"

B. HAMLET DARWIN
"Bromius! Iacchus! Son of Zeus!"

PATRONS, WAITERS, ETC.

"He's drunk."

"Greek gods!—does he think we don't know he's a Methodist?"

"This is no time for blasphemy!"

"A little learning goes to the heads of fools."

"Yes, drink deep of the Pierian spring or . . ."

"Very picturesque though, 'Bromius! Iacchus!' very picturesque."

B. HAMLET DARWIN

"'O esca vermium! O massa pulveris!' Where is the rich Dives? He who was always eating? He is no longer even eaten."

PATRONS, WAITERS, ETC.

"A riddle! A riddle!"

"He is looking for a friend."

"He has lost something. Tell him to look under the table."

MESSENGER

"He means the worms have eaten Dives; and that, in their turn dead, the worms have been eaten by other worms."

B. HAMLET DARWIN

"Or quick tell me where has gone Samson?—strongest of men. He is no longer even weak. And where, oh tell me, where is the beautiful Appollon? He is no longer even ugly. And where are the snows of yesteryear? And where is Tom Giles? Bill Taylor? Jake Holtz? In other words, 'Here today and gone tomorrow.'"

MESSENGER

"Yes, what he says is but too true. An incident such as the sad demise we are now considering makes one stop 'midst the hustle-bustle of our work-a-day world to ponder the words of the poet who says we are 'nourriture des vers!' Continue, dear brother in sorrow, we attend your every word."

B. HAMLET DARWIN

"I shall begin all over again, folks.

"While I sit laughing with my friends, a messenger stalks into the café. He cries: 'Beagle! Beagle! Janey has killed herself!' I jump up, white as a sheet of paper, let us say, and shriek in anguish: 'Bromius! Iacchus! Son of Zeus!' You then demand why I call so loudly on Dionysius. I go into my routine.

"Dionysius! Dionysius! I call on the wine-god because his begetting and birth were so different from Janey's, so different from yours, so different from mine. I call on Dionysius in order to explain the tragedy. A tragedy that is not alone Janey's, but one that is the tragedy of all of us.

"Who among us can boast that he was born three times, as was Dionysius?—once from the womb of 'hapless Semele,' once from the thigh of Zeus, and once from the flames. Or who can say, like Christ, that he was born of a virgin? Or who can even claim to have been born as was Gargantua? Alas! none of us. Yet it is necessary for us to compete—as it was necessary for Janey to compete—with Dionysius the thrice born, Christ son of God, Gargantua born 'midst a torrent of tripe at a most memorable party. You hear the thunder, you see the lightning, you smell the forests, you drink wine—and you attempt to be as was Christ, Dionysius, Gargantua! You who were born from the womb, covered with slime and foul blood, 'midst cries of anguish and suffering.

"At your birth, instead of the Three Kings, the Dove, the Star of Bethlehem, there was only old Doctor Haasen-schweitz who wore rubber gloves and carried a towel over his arm like a waiter.

"And how did the lover, your father, come to his beloved? [After a warm day in the office he had seen two dogs in the street.] Did he come in the shape of a swan, a bull, or a shower of gold? No! But with his pants unsup-ported by braces, came he from the bath-room." . . .

B. Hamlet Darwin towered over his glass of cognac, and, in the theatre of his mind, over a cringing audience— tempestuous, gallant, headstrong, lovable Beagle Dionysius Hamlet Darwin. Up into his giant heart there welled a profound feeling of love for humanity. He choked with emotion as he realized the truth of his observations. Terrible indeed was the competition in which his hearers spent their lives; a competition that demanded their being more than animals.

He raised his hand as though to bless them, and the cus-tomers and waiters were silent. Gently, yet with a sense of mighty love, he murmured, "Ah my children." Then, sweeping the Café Carcas with tear-dimmed, eagle's eyes, he cried: "Yet, ah yet, are you expected to compete with Christ whose father is God, with Dionysius whose father is God; you who were Janey Davenport, or one conceived in an offhand manner on a rainy afternoon."

"Cognac! Cognac!"

After building up his tear-jerker routine for a repeat, he blacked out and went into his juggling for the curtain. He climaxed the finale by keeping in the air an Ivory Tower, a

Still White Bird, the Holy Grail, the Nails, the Scourge, the Thorns, and a piece of the True Cross.

Yours,

Beagle

"Well, what do you think of them?"

Balso awoke and saw Miss McGeeney, the biographer of Samuel Perkins, sitting beside him at the café table.

"Think of what?"

"The two letters you just read," Miss McGeeney said impatiently. "They form part of a novel I'm writing in the manner of Richardson. Give me your candid opinion: do you think the epistolary style too old-fashioned?"

Refreshed by the nap he had taken, Balso examined his interrogator with interest. She was a fine figure of a woman. He wanted to please her and said:

"A stormy wind blows through your pages, sweeping the reader breathless . . . witchery and madness. Comparable to George Bernard Shaw. It is a drama of passion that has all the appeal of wild living and the open road. Comparable to George Bernard Shaw. There's magic in its pages, and warm strong sympathy for an alien race."

"Thank you," she said with precision.

How gracious is a woman grateful, thought Balso. He felt young again: the heel of a loaf, a piece of cheese, a bottle of wine and an apple. Clear speakers, naked in the sun. Young students: and the days are very full, and the nights burst with excitement, and life is a torrent roaring.

"Oh!" Balso exclaimed, carried away by these memories of his youth. "Oh!" His mouth formed an O with lips torn angry in laying duck's eggs from a chicken's rectum.

"Oh, what?" Miss McGeeney was obviously annoyed.

"Oh, I loved a girl once. All day she did nothing but place bits of meat on the petals of flowers. She choked the rose with butter and cake crumbs, soiling the crispness of its dainty petals with gravy and cheese. She wanted the rose to attract flies, not butterflies or bees. She wanted to make of her garden a . . ."

"Balso! Balso! Is it you?" cried Miss McGeeney, spilling what was left of his beer, much to the disgust of the waiter who hovered near.

"Balso! Balso! Is it you?" she cried again before he could answer. "Don't you recognize me? I'm Mary. Mary McGeeney, your old sweetheart."

Balso realized that she was indeed Mary. Changed, alas! but with much of the old Mary left, particularly about the eyes. No longer was she dry and stick-like, but a woman, warmly moist.

They sat and devoured each other with looks until the waiter suggested that they leave as he wanted to close the place and go home.

They left arm-in-arm, walking as in a dream. Balso did the steering and they soon found themselves behind a thick clump of bushes. Miss McGeeney lay down on her back with her hands behind her head and her knees wide apart. Balso stood over her and began a speech the intent of which was obvious.

"First," he said, "let us consider the political aspect. You who talk of Liberty and cling to the protection of Dogma in the face of Life and the Army of Unutterable Physical Law, cast, I say, cast free the anchors, let go the moorings of your desires! Let to the breezes flap the standard of your revolt!

"Also we must consider the philosophical aspects of the proposed act. Nature has lent you for a brief time a few organs capable of giving pleasure. Among these are to be

listed the sexual ones. The organs of sex offer in reward for
their intelligent use a very intense type of pleasure.
Pleasure, it is necessary to admit, is the only good. It is only
reasonable to say that if pleasure is desirable—and who
besides a few fanatics say it is not?—one should get all the
pleasure possible. First it is important to dissociate certain
commonplace ideas. As a thinking person, as an individu-
alist—and you are both of these, are you not, love?—it is
necessary to dissociate the idea of pleasure from that of
generation. Furthermore, it is necessary to disregard one's
unreasonable moral training. Sex, not marriage, is a sacra-
ment. You admit it? Then why allow an ancient, inherited
code to foist on you, a thinking being, the old, outmoded
strictures? Sexual acts are not sins, errors, faults, weak-
nesses. The sexual acts give pleasure, and pleasure is desirable. So come, Mary, let us have some fun.

"And for the sake of Art, Mary. You desire to write, do
you not, love? And you must admit that without knowing
what all the shooting is about, a sincere artist is badly
handicapped. How can you portray men if you have never
known a man? How can you read and understand, see and
understand, without ever having known the divine excitement? How can you hope to motivate a theft, a murder, a
rape, a suicide, convincingly? And are you ever out of
themes? In my bed, love, you will find new themes, new
interpretations, new experiences. You will be able to judge
for yourself whether love is only three minutes of rapture
followed by a feeling of profound disgust, or the all-con-
suming fire, the divine principle, a foretaste of the joys of
heaven? Come, Mary McGeeney, to bed and a new world.

"And now, finally, we come to the Time-argument. Do
not confuse what I shall say under this head with the the-
ories so much in vogue among the metaphysicians and
physicists, those weavers of the wind. My 'Time' is that of

the poets. In a little while, love, you will be dead; that is my burden. In a little while, we all will be dead. Golden lads and chimney-sweeps, all dead. And when dying, will you be able to say, I turn down an empty glass, having drunk to the full, lived to the full? Is it not madness to deny life? Hurry! Hurry! for all is soon over. Blown, O rose! in the morning, thou shalt fade ere noon. Do you realize the tune the clock is playing? The seconds, how they fly! All is soon over! All is soon over! Let us snatch, while yet we may, in this brief span, whose briefness merely gilds the bubble so soon destroyed, some few delights. Have you thought of the grave? O love! have you thought of the grave and of the change that shall come over your fair body? Your most beautiful bride—though now she be pleasant and sweet to the nose—will be damnably mouldy a hundred years hence. O how small a part of time they share, that are so wonderous sweet and fair. Ah, make the most of what we yet may spend before we too into the dust descend. Into the dust, Mary! Thy sweet plenty, in the dust. I tremble, I burn for thy sweet embrace. Be not miserly with thy white flesh. Give your gracious body, for such a short time lent you. Give, for in the giving you shall receive and still have what you give. Only time can rob you of your flesh, I cannot. And time will rob you—it will, it will! And those who husbanded the golden grain, and those who flung it to the wind like rain . . .”

Here Balso threw himself to the ground beside his beloved.

How did she receive him? At first, by saying no.

No. No! Innocent, confused. Oh Balso! Oh Balso! with pictures of the old farm house, old pump, old folks at home, and the old oaken bucket—ivy over all.

Sir! Stamping her tiny foot—imperative, irate. Sir, how dare you, sir! Do you presume? Down, Rover, I say down!

The prying thumbs of insolent chauffeurs. The queen chooses. Elizabeth of England, Catherine of Russia, Faustina of Rome.

These two noes graded into two yes-and-noes.

No . . . Oh . . . Oh, no. Eyes aswim with tears. Voice throaty, husky with repressed passion. Oh, how sweet, sweetheart, sweetheart, sweetheart. Oh, I'm melting. My very bones are liquid. I'll swoon if you don't leave me alone. Leave me alone, I'm dizzy. No . . . No! You beast!

No: No, Balso, not tonight. No, not tonight. No! I'm sorry, Balso, but not tonight. Some other time, perhaps yes, but not tonight. Please be a dear, not tonight. Please!

But Balso would not take no for an answer, and he soon obtained the following yeses:

Allowing hot breath to escape from between moist, open lips: eyes upset, murmurs love. Tiger skin on divan. Spanish shawl on grand piano. Altar of Love. Church and Brothel. Odors of Ind and Afric. There's Egypt in your eyes. Rich, opulent love; beautiful, tapestried love; oriental, perfumed love.

Hard-bitten. Casual. Smart. Been there before. I've had policemen. No trace of a feminine whimper. Decidedly revisiting well-known, well-plowed ground. No new trees, wells, or even fences.

Desperate for life. Live! Experience! Live one's own. Your body is an instrument, an organ or a drum. Harmony. Order. Breasts. The apple of my eye, the pear of my abdomen. What is life without love? I burn! I ache! Hurrah!

Moooompitcher yaaaah. Oh I never hoped to know the passion, the sensuality hidden within you—yes, yes. Drag me down into the mire, drag. Yes! And with your hair the lust from my eyes brush. Yes . . . Yes . . . Ooh! Ah!

The miracle was made manifest. The Two became One. The One that is all things and yet no one of them: the priest and the god, the immolation, the sacrificial rite, the libation offered to ancestors, the incantation, the sacrificial egg, the altar, the ego and the alter ego, as well as the father, the child, and the grandfather of the universe, the mystic doctrine, the purification, the syllable "Om," the path, the master, the witness, the receptacle, the Spirit of Public School 186, the last ferry that leaves for Weehawken at seven.

His body broke free of the bard. It took on a life of its own; a life that knew nothing of the poet Balso. Only to death can this release be likened—to the mechanics of decay. After death the body takes command; it performs the manual of disintegration with a marvelous certainty. So now, his body performed the evolutions of love with a like sureness.

In this activity, Home and Duty, Love and Art, were forgotten.

An army moved in his body, an eager army of hurrying sensations. These sensations marched at first methodically and then hysterically, but always with precision. The army of his body commenced a long intricate drill, a long involved ceremony. A ceremony whose ritual unwound and manoeuvred itself with the confidence and training of chemicals acting under the stimulus of a catalytic agent.

His body screamed and shouted as it marched and uncoiled; then, with one heaving shout of triumph, it fell back quiet.

The army that a moment before had been thundering in his body retreated slowly—victorious, relieved.